Ro
a
Grimmond

SHIRLEY ISHERWOOD

Illustrated by Jean Baylis

Beaver Books

Also available in Beaver by Shirley Isherwood
Something New for a Bear to do
A Special Place for Edward James

A Beaver Book

Published by Arrow Books Limited
20 Vauxhall Bridge Road
London SW1V 2SA

An imprint of Random Century Group

London Melbourne Sydney Auckland
Johannesburg and agencies throughout the world

First published in 1988 by Hutchinson Children's Books

Beaver edition 1989

Set in Baskerville by Deltatype Ltd,
Ellesmere Port, Cheshire
Made and printed in Great Britain by
Cox & Wyman Ltd, Reading

ISBN 0 09 963730 8

Contents

For Alexander Mark Caplan

The arrival of Grimmond

Robert had a pair of beautiful red boots. In the morning, he put them on and went down the stairs, clump-clump-clump. 'Here comes Robert-The-Boot!' said his family.

Robert wore his red boots every day. At night he took them off, and put them side by side on the rug. Then he lay in bed, and gazed at the little door in the ceiling. The little door was the door to the loft. Suitcases, boxes and old pictures were kept there. It was a very mysterious place.

Robert thought that wild beasts lived in the loft. He didn't know what they looked like, and he didn't know their names. He didn't think that they were tigers, because tigers growl and roar. The beasts in the loft were very quiet. They made little rustling noises in the night, and sometimes they talked to one another, in whispers.

Every night, the beasts in the loft prowled about – until one day, when Robert found a secret friend. He was called Grimmond, he said, and he had come to live in the loft. He brought his bed, with a patchwork quilt, and he trundled it up the path to the house. The brass knobs shone in the sun. Robert lay on his back, in the grass, and laughed and kicked his red boots in the air. For no one but Robert could see Grimmond – not even Robert's sister Maud. Grimmond could come to tea, or lie on the living-room rug, and no one would know that he was there.

When Grimmond came to live in the loft, he said that he would make all the wild beasts go away. He stood on the end of Robert's bed, and opened the door of the loft with his umbrella. 'All tigers begone!' he said, in a stern voice.

'I don't think they're called tigers,' said Robert.

So Grimmond waved his umbrella, and cried, 'All bears begone!'

'I don't think they're called bears,' said Robert.

'Are they called elephants?' asked Grimmond.

Robert shook his head. 'I don't think they've got a name,' he said.

Grimmond said that everything and everyone had a name – then, when you said the name,

everyone knew who or what you were talking about.

Robert said that perhaps the beasts in the loft were called Creepers and Murmurers, because that's what they did; they crept about and murmured to one another.

So Grimmond scrambled up into the loft. Robert watched as first his head, and then his legs and paws disappeared through the little door. Then he sat down on his bed, and waited. He waited for a long time, and then he called, 'Grimmond,' very softly. 'Grimmond, are you there?'

Grimmond's face appeared in the doorway of

the loft. 'There are no Creepers and Murmurers here,' he said. 'Only boxes, and suitcases, and some old newspaper flapping about.'

That night, as Robert lay in bed, he listened for the sound of the beasts in the loft – but there was nothing to be heard; only the sound of the wind, as it blew through a little hole in the roof, the sound of the rustling newspapers, and the sound of Grimmond's voice, saying, 'Goodnight, sleep tight. Goodnight, Robert-The-Boot!'

The yellow telephone

Robert-The-Boot was sitting on the bottom stair, waiting for a phone call from his grandmother. Grimmond sat beside him. Grimmond had never had a phone call. The thought made him very sad – and the more he thought about never having had a phone call, the sadder he became. He pulled his woolly hat down over his eyes, and sighed. He sighed so much that Robert said that he could share the phone call from Robert's grandmother.

Grimmond said, 'Thank you. But it isn't like having a phone call of your very own.' Then he sighed again, so hard that he fell off the stair and lay on the floor. 'I want someone to ring me up,' he said. 'I want a yellow telephone, with a bell that goes BRIIIIINK!'

'Please get up,' said Robert – but Grimmond didn't move. He lay there as people passed up and down the hall. Robert's mother had to Hoover round him very carefully, which was difficult, as she couldn't tell exactly where he was. Grimmond didn't move, not even when the Hoover pulled his woolly hat off.

He didn't move when Robert's grandmother telephoned.

He didn't move when Maud wheeled her bicycle in through the front door and up the hall. She wheeled it very carefully, even though she didn't really believe that Grimmond was lying there in the hall. She pretended to see him, but

Robert knew that she was only pretending, because she said, 'Oh yes, I see him. I like his hat!'

'His hat's in the *Hoover*!' shouted Robert.

For the rest of the day, Grimmond lay in the hall.

When evening came, Robert climbed up the stairs to bed. As he went, he thought of Grimmond lying sadly in the hall. And then – just as he was about to take off his red boots – he remembered his toy telephone. It was yellow, and it had a bell that rang very loudly.

Grimmond was very pleased. He carried the toy telephone up to the loft, then he leaned out from the little door to say, 'Goodnight, sleep tight! Goodnight, Robert-The-Boot.'

But it was a long time before Robert could fall asleep. Grimmond got telephone calls all through the night – from his sisters and grandma and his grandpa, his cousins and his aunts.

Mud!

One morning, Robert went out to play. It had
been raining hard, and down at the bottom of the
garden was a big patch of black, sticky mud.
Splodge-splodge-splodge! through the mud went
Robert, in his beautiful red boots. Great splashes
of mud went everywhere – on his face, on his
hands, on his clothes and his hair.

Grimmond sat on a branch of the tree, and
watched him.

'Come and play,' said Robert.

But Grimmond just shook his head. 'Grimmonds don't really like mud,' he said.

After a while Maud came down the path. 'Ah-
ha!' she said, when she saw Robert. Then she took
a deep breath, and shouted as loudly as she could,

'ROBERT IS PLAYING IN THE MUD!'

Maud could shout louder than anyone else in the world. Her mother heard her in the kitchen, and came to the door. She looked down the path, and saw Robert. 'Oh, Robert!' she said. 'How dirty you are!'

'Grimmond is quite dirty too,' said Maud.

'No, he isn't,' said Robert – for he knew that Maud couldn't see how Grimmond was sitting on the branch, as clean and green as the new leaves on the tree. Somehow, Grimmond never seemed to get dirty.

Robert's mother said that he must have a bath. She took off his muddy clothes, and put them into the laundry basket. Then she took his muddy

boots downstairs to clean them.

Robert sat in the bath, with his three sailing ships. Grimmond sat on the edge of the bath, and made waves in the water, so that the ships would bob up and down. Then he made the waves so big that they splashed right over the edge of the bath.

Maud brought some warm, dry towels into the bathroom – but she couldn't see how Grimmond was making a wonderful storm at sea in the bath. All she saw was Robert, and the pools of water on the floor.

'Ah-ha!' said Maud, when she saw the puddles, and she went out of the bathroom, humming a little tune under her breath.

'Maud never makes puddles on the floor when she has a bath,' said Robert.

'Maud never has a storm at sea,' said Grimmond.

Robert rubbed some soap on his sponge, and began to wash his neck. Grimmond looked at himself in the bathroom mirror. 'I think I am very handsome,' he said. 'I wonder if I would be *more* handsome if I grew a beard?' Then – because he could do anything at all – he grew a thick, red, curly beard, and then a short, black, gleaming beard. But he didn't like either of them, and after gazing at himself for a little while longer, he made them disappear. He sat down on the laundry basket, and looked at the water in the bath. It lay still, and smooth and shiny. The three ships rocked to and fro by the big, silvery taps. 'We'll just make some very small waves,' said Grimmond. 'So that your ships can go on a voyage.'

He dabbled his hand in the bath, and the little sparkling waves ran up the bath. Then bigger and bigger they came. WOOSH! SPLASH! they went, over the side of the bath. 'All hands on deck!' cried Grimmond, as the ships crashed against the sponge.

When the storm was over, Robert and Grimmond looked at the puddles on the floor. They were very big, and there were a lot of them. Grimmond mopped them up with a towel, and hung the towel on the rack to dry. 'No one will ever know,' he said – and, quick as a flash, he disappeared.

'Oh, Robert!' said Robert's mother, when she came into the bathroom, and saw the shiny, wet floor.

'Grimmond did it,' said Robert. Then he put on his dry clothes, and his red boots, and went out into the garden, to find where Grimmond was hiding himself.

Grimmond was hiding in a tree, but Robert found him very quickly; for the sun was now shining, and it shone through the leaves on the trees, and on the brass buttons on Grimmond's coat.

The dragon in the cupboard

It was some time since Grimmond had come to live with Robert. All the noises in the loft had stopped, except for the twanging of the springs when Grimmond climbed into bed, and, sometimes, the ringing of his yellow telephone. But suddenly strange little noises began to be heard in the cupboard under the stairs. At first they were so faint that Robert couldn't be sure if he heard them at all. But, little by little, they became louder. Grimmond heard them too. 'Sometimes, things get into one's cupboard, and live there,' he said.

'What sort of things?' asked Robert. But Grimmond wouldn't say, and went off down the garden path, swinging his umbrella.

Robert didn't like the noises in the cupboard. They made him feel a little bit afraid. It is strange how a noise in a cupboard can frighten one person, while another person cares not at all, and goes off with their hat at a jaunty angle. Robert watched until Grimmond had almost reached the bottom of the garden; then he ran after him. 'Please go and see who is living in the cupboard,' he said.

'Very well,' said Grimmond, and he hung his umbrella from a branch of the tree, went back into the house, and flung open the cupboard door. 'Whoever is living in there, come out at once!' he said, in his stern voice.

At first there was nothing to be heard. Then there came a soft little scrabbling sound, like the sound of an animal turning round and round in its nest. Robert stepped back from the cupboard door – for he was still feeling a bit afraid. But Grimmond just marched into the cupboard, and cried, 'Ha-ha!'

'Ho-hum,' answered the voice, from the back of the cupboard.

'Whatever it is, it is just waking up,' said Grimmond. 'And that is the best time to catch something, when it is just waking up.' He began to fling out brushes and mops, dusters and tins of polish, as deeper and deeper into the cupboard he went.

The dweller in the cupboard was completely awakened by the noise. 'HOO!' it cried.

Robert stood against the wall of the passage, and held his breath. He was still feeling afraid, but he had also begun to feel quite curious.

It is interesting to have two feelings at the same time – but it is also rather puzzling when you don't know which one you are feeling the most. Robert wanted to run away, but he also wanted to find out who was saying 'HOO!' in the cupboard. And so he danced from foot to foot, while from inside the cupboard there came the skittering sound of claws on wooden floorboards. A moment later, there tumbled out into the passage a small, fat, pink dragon. He blinked in the sudden light, rubbed his eyes with his two plump paws, then ran out into the garden. Grimmond came hurrying from the cupboard and ran after him. Robert ran after Grimmond.

Round and round the garden they went. The small pink dragon was so plump that he waddled as he ran – which made Robert laugh. But sometimes he stopped and turned and cried 'HOO!' very loudly – which made Grimmond and Robert stop too, and stare at him in a thoughtful way. 'He's quite a small dragon,' said Grimmond. 'But sometimes small things can be very fierce.'

As they stood, the small dragon ran off again, and Robert and Grimmond lost sight of him in the long grass.

Robert and Grimmond sat down to rest. 'What I am wondering', said Grimmond, as they sat, 'is, *has he brought any relations with him?*'

'Relations?' said Robert.

'Brothers, or cousins or aunts,' said Grimmond. 'Big, fierce relations, who look after him.'

The thought that the small dragon might have big, fierce relations made Robert begin to feel afraid again. A small, pink, waddling dragon is one thing – but full-grown dragons are quite another.

'Let's go back into the house,' said Robert. 'Perhaps he'll go away.'

But Grimmond shook his head at this. 'Once you have seen your dragon, you must catch him,' he said; and he got to his feet and went off through the grass, green and brave, and with his hat still at its jaunty angle. Suddenly, up jumped the small dragon, and made off down the path. Grimmond and Robert ran after him, to the bottom of the garden, where the small dragon ran inside a bush. Which was a mistake; for while there was a way into the bush, made by the arching branches, there was no way out again.

Robert and Grimmond sat down in front of the bush, and looked at the small dragon. 'Hoo,' he said – but his heart was no longer in it, for he was tired, and ready for his mid-morning nap.

Now that Robert saw him close to, he could tell that the dragon was really only a baby. His tummy was as round as a puppy's, and when he tried to breathe fire, nothing came out of his mouth but spit-bubbles. He turned round and round in the space inside the bush. Then he lay down, put his nose on his pink paws, and went to sleep.

'What shall we do with him?' asked Robert.

'I'd rather like to keep him,' said Grimmond – then he looked hard at Robert, for he knew that Robert had been frightened. 'He is only a very *little* dragon,' he said.

'Well, I was only a little bit afraid,' said Robert.

So that is how the small, pink dragon came to live with Robert and Grimmond. He made his home in the bush, and came and went just as he pleased. Sometimes Robert and Grimmond didn't see him for days; but he always returned when they least expected him, jumping up suddenly from the long grass, crying 'HOO!' and blowing his spit-bubbles.

A jolly uncle

One day, Robert's uncle came to tea. He was a very large and jolly uncle. He sat Robert on his knee, and bounced him up and down. Robert didn't like it very much – but his uncle seemed to like bouncing him, so he sat as politely as he could. Then, 'Thank you very much,' he said, 'but I would like to stop now.'

He tumbled down from his uncle's knee, and crept under the table, where Grimmond was sitting with his woolly hat pulled down over his eyes. 'Has he gone,' asked Grimmond.

'No,' said Robert.

As he spoke, the corner of the tablecloth was lifted, and the big, smiling face of his uncle appeared. 'Well, well, well!' he said. 'What's all this?' And he held out his empty hand, felt behind Robert's ear, and brought out a shining five-penny piece. Robert was very pleased.

'Shall I do it again?' asked his uncle.

'Yes, please!' said Robert, and he scrambled from beneath the table, and stood by his uncle's knee. Robert's uncle felt behind Robert's right ear, and brought out another five-penny piece.

'Thank you!' said Robert, and he went back under the table to show Grimmond.

But Grimmond just sniffed, and pulled his hat further down over his eyes. 'What's the matter?' asked Robert.

'Nothing,' said Grimmond. But something *was*

the matter; he looked greener and smaller – so small that he seemed to be disappearing beneath his hat.

'Please don't go!' said Robert – for he knew that Grimmond could do any magical thing he wished. He could make himself as big as a house . . . or he could vanish altogether.

'Don't go,' he said again – but Grimmond just became smaller and smaller.

'You don't want me any more,' he said, 'now that you've got a magical uncle.'

He made himself so tiny that his voice could hardly be heard. 'Bouncing uncle . . . magical uncle . . . pennies behind the ears. . . .' Robert heard him say, before he vanished completely, leaving behind his woolly hat with the tassel.

'Please come back!' said Robert. 'It isn't magic. It's a trick.'

'A trick?' said Grimmond, coming back at once, and putting his hat back on. 'Are you sure?'

'Of course,' said Robert, and he took one of the five-penny pieces and held it between his fingers. He held it by the edge, so that when Grimmond looked at the palm of his hand, the five-penny piece could hardly be seen. Then he turned his hand round, so that Grimmond could see the coin sticking out at the back.

Grimmond took the coin, and held it in his paw, just as Robert had done. Then, very gently, he felt behind Robert's ear, and brought the coin out. He was very pleased with himself, and he did the trick six times before he gave the money back to Robert. Then he took Robert on his knee, and bounced him up and down, as Robert's uncle had done.

'Thank you,' said Robert. 'Thank you very much, thank you very much indeed!'

Then he lay on his back and laughed – for he knew that even though his uncle was peering under the table, he couldn't see how Grimmond was sitting and bringing pennies from behind his ears . . . hundreds of pennies . . . thousands of pennies . . . hundreds and thousands, and millions of pennies!

A cold in the head

One morning, Robert woke up with a cold in the head. His nose was running, and his throat felt prickly and sore. 'You'll have to stay in bed today,' said his mother, and she brought him a hot lemon drink, with honey in it.

Grimmond sat on Robert's pillow. 'I've got a cold in the head, too,' he said. So Robert gave him some of the lemon drink. Grimmond drank quite a lot of it, then scraped out all the honey which had settled on the bottom of the mug, with his paw. 'What do you do when you have a cold in the head?' he asked, cheerfully.

'You stay in bed,' said Robert.

'Oh,' said Grimmond. Then, 'I think that perhaps I haven't got a cold after all,' he said –

and he jumped off the bed, and ran from the room, waving goodbye with his sticky, green paw. Robert heard his feet go pitter-pat as he ran down the stairs.

Robert got out of bed, and went to the window. Grimmond and the small, pink dragon were walking across the lawn. Grimmond was swinging his umbrella, and the small dragon was waving his tail. Their two heads were close together, as though they were planning to do something wonderful and exciting.

Robert went sadly back to bed. It is impossible to do wonderful and exciting things when you have a cold in the head. His mother brought him

some books, his crayons, and a jigsaw on a tray. But Robert didn't want any of these things. What he wanted was to be out in the sunny garden, with Grimmond and the small dragon. He lay back on his pillow, and wondered what they were doing. As he lay and wondered, he fell fast asleep. He didn't wake up until lunch time, when his mother brought him a bowl of soup.

After he had eaten the soup, Robert felt a little better. He got out of bed, and went to the window, to see what Grimmond and the small dragon were doing. They were sitting in the bush, but Robert could see the shining buttons on Grimmond's jacket, and the tip of the small dragon's pink tail.

Robert waved to them – but before Grimmond or the small dragon could look out of the bush and see him, Maud came into the room. 'GET BACK INTO BED AT ONCE!' she said, in her loud, bossy voice.

Robert got into bed, and Maud tucked the sheets and blankets round him so tightly that he could scarcely move. 'Thank you very much,' he said. But as soon as Maud left the room, he wriggled and wriggled until the bedclothes came loose. Then he got out of bed, and went to the window.

Grimmond and the small dragon were sitting side by side on the lowest branch of the tree. Grimmond looked quite happy, but the small

dragon was clinging to the branch with the claws
of his four paws, and Robert knew that he was
feeling a little nervous. The small dragon had
never flown as high as the branch of the tree
before. Robert wished that he could have been
there to see him do it. He waved and waved, but
neither the small dragon nor Grimmond saw him.
Grimmond was busy patting the small dragon on
the head, and saying, 'Well done!' And as for the
small dragon himself, when you have done something as wonderful as flying up into a tree for the
first time, you are far too excited to think of
someone with a cold in the head.

Robert went back to bed, and lay listening to

the sounds of the house and garden. Everyone was busy and happy doing something, and Grimmond and the small dragon had forgotten all about him. Perhaps now that the small dragon had learned how to use his wings, he would fly away, thought Robert, and perhaps Grimmond would go with him. The more that Robert thought of this, the more sure he became that this is what would happen. He lay very still, and listened for the sound of Grimmond's voice, or the sound of the dragon blowing spit-bubbles. But nothing at all could be heard now from the garden.

'Grimmond's gone away!' Robert said, when his mother brought his tea.

'No, he hasn't,' said his mother. 'Why, I can see him, sitting at the foot of your bed.'

But Robert knew that his mother had never seen Grimmond, and that Grimmond wasn't sitting on the bed. He had gone to have a great adventure with the small dragon. Robert ate some of his tea, and then he lay down under the bedclothes. His head felt heavy, and he had just time for one sad thought about Grimmond and the dragon, before he fell asleep.

When he awoke, the room had grown darker, and there was a strange little whispering sound from under his bed. Robert leant over to look – and there they were, Grimmond and the small dragon curled up together, with the dragon's head on Grimmond's knee. Grimmond was telling a story about the small dragon's great-grandfather.

It was a wonderful story, about how he once flew over the tops of the trees, with his green and gold scales flashing in the sun. Robert curled up beneath his blankets, and lay as still as a mouse, and listened. But before Grimmond could finish the story, he fell fast asleep once more.

It was morning when he woke again. The sun was shining, and his cold was almost gone. He felt very happy. 'Grimmond!' he shouted. 'Tell me the story about the dragon's great-grandfather!'

But it was a sad little voice that answered him from the loft. 'I'm afraid I can't,' croaked Grimmond. 'I've caught a cold in the head.'

Harry, a moose and a mouse

Robert had a pet, a white mouse called Harry. He lived in a cage, with straw on the floor, and little dishes for food and water.

Robert took great care of Harry. Every day he cleaned out the cage, and put in fresh food and water; and he talked to his pet. He held him gently in the palm of his hand, and said, 'Hallo, Harry. How are you today?'

Every morning, Grimmond sat quietly and watched all this – until one day, when he said, '*I* want a pet. I want a pet of my own.'

'What kind of pet would you like?' asked Robert. 'A cat? A dog?'

Grimmond shook his head. 'I want a giraffe,' he said.

'Oh, Grimmond,' said Robert. 'A giraffe isn't a pet.'

'Yes it is,' said Grimmond. 'A giraffe is a lovely pet.'

Straight away he conjured up a giraffe, and it stood there on the lawn, on its four long legs, and with its long neck swaying from side to side as it looked around the garden. 'Come along!' said Grimmond. 'It's time for a walk!'

The giraffe just turned and plodded slowly over the garden, and began to eat the leaves of the trees and bushes. 'Stop him!' cried Robert – but the giraffe just went on eating. Soon all the leaves had vanished from the tops of the trees, and the bare branches stuck out in a very odd way indeed.

'Stop eating the garden!' shouted Robert. But the giraffe just lowered his long neck over the garden next door, and went on munching.

'All giraffes eat a lot,' said Grimmond. 'He'll stop soon.'

But the giraffe didn't stop. When he had eaten all the leaves in the next door garden, he stepped over the fences, and began to eat the leaves in the garden next door but one.

'What shall I do?' asked Grimmond, as he watched his giraffe going from garden to garden, eating all the leaves of the trees. He looked so small and green, and unhappy, that Robert ran into the house, to ask Maud if she knew what to do

33

with a giraffe who wouldn't stop eating gardens. (Maud was very bossy, and she shouted very loudly, but sometimes she had good ideas.)

Maud was sitting at the kitchen table, painting a picture of a cat. 'Maud,' said Robert, quietly. 'Grimmond has got a giraffe.'

'Has he?' said Maud. She didn't seem very interested, and went on painting the cat's whiskers, very carefully with the tip of her brush.

'It's a nice giraffe,' said Robert. 'But it's a bit big.'

'Is it?' said Maud, smiling at her picture.

'It's eating all the garden,' said Robert.

'*Is it?*' said Maud, and she jumped up at once, and ran outside. 'CHANGE THAT GIRAFFE

INTO SOMETHING ELSE!' she shouted.

Poor Grimmond was so startled by this sudden shout that he changed his giraffe into a very large animal. It wasn't as tall as the giraffe, but it was certainly big, and it came roaring and bellowing through the garden, tossing its antlers. 'It's a moose!' said Robert.

'WELL, HE CAN'T HAVE A MOOSE EITHER!' shouted Maud, and she stamped back into the house.

'I'm sorry,' said Grimmond. 'What I meant was a *mouse*.' The moose vanished, and Grimmond held out his paw, on which rested a small, white mouse. He was a nice little animal. His nose was pink, and his whiskers twitched. Grimmond sat and gazed at him. 'If only he was bigger . . .,' he said – and before Robert could stop him, he made the mouse as big as a house.

'Oh, Grimmond!' said Robert. 'Now he's too big to be a pet. Where will he live?'

'In a large cage,' said Grimmond.

'And what will he eat?' asked Robert.

'Cheese,' said Grimmond, '. . . a lot of cheese.'

With a sigh, he changed the mouse back to its proper size, and carried him to the mouse-cage.

Grimmond grew very fond of his mouse. He called him Albert, and Albert lived happily with Robert's mouse, Harry, until they both became very old mice, and died.

Climbing

James lived next door to Robert. He was two years older than Robert; he was taller and stronger; and he was very good at climbing trees. Robert wanted very much to be just like James.

One day, when Robert, Grimmond and the small pink dragon were sitting on the front door step, they saw James go striding down his garden path. When he reached the bottom of the garden, he climbed the tree. Up he went from branch to branch, as quick and as nimble as a squirrel. Then he climbed back again, and went whistling down the street. 'I wish I could climb trees like James,' said Robert.

Grimmond took Robert's hand in his paw, and led him down the garden path. 'But it is very easy,' he said, as they went. 'First you climb up to the lowest branch. Then you climb on to the next branch. Then up you go, until you reach the top.'

Robert stood at the foot of the tree, and looked up into the branches. It was a very tall tree, and the top seemed almost to touch the sky. 'Could I really climb it?' he asked.

'Of course you could!' said Grimmond. The small dragon, who had followed them down the path, scampered round in circles, and blew a lot of spit-bubbles. Grimmond patted his head, to calm him. 'He says that he's very excited at the thought of you climbing the tree,' said Grimmond.

Robert himself felt quite excited; there was a fluttering feeling in his tummy. But he grasped the stout tree trunk with both his arms, scrambled about with his feet until he found a place to put his toes; then up he went, to the lowest branch.

It was wonderful. 'I'm just like James!' he said, as he sat on the branch, swinging his feet. Grimmond climbed up, and sat down at Robert's side.

'But James climbs higher,' he said.

Robert stood up, took hold of the next branch, and very carefully pulled himself up until he sat in the fork of the tree. Grimmond climbed up after him. Below, in the garden, the small, pink dragon tried to fly up to the lowest branch. He ran over the lawn, flung himself into the air, and then came down – FLUMP! – in the grass, for he still hadn't learned how to use his wings properly and only once had he managed to fly up into the tree.

Robert laughed. 'He wants to be like his great-grandfather,' he said. He knew how the small dragon felt. '*I* want to be like James,' he said. He felt very happy, for it was lovely to sit in the fork of the tree, like a bird safe in its nest. But Grimmond just looked at him. 'James climbs much higher than this,' he said.

So Robert climbed up to the next branch. It was very high, and it didn't feel as safe as the fork of the tree, for it swayed up and down when

Robert sat on it. At the foot of the tree, he could see the small dragon gazing up at him in wonder. He seemed very small and pink, and everything else in the garden seemed small and very far away. 'Grimmond,' said Robert, 'I think I would like to go down now.'

But, while climbing up a tree can seem very hard, climbing down again can be even harder. Every time that Robert looked at the branches below him he felt dizzy.

'Down you come!' said Grimmond, cheerfully.

'Grimmond . . . I can't!' said poor Robert.

'Yes, you can,' said Grimmond, firmly. 'If you were brave enough to climb up the tree, you can be brave enough to climb down again. Hold the branch tightly with your paws; then step down on to the next branch.'

Holding tight to the branch, Robert felt for the branch below him. When both his red boots were firmly on it, he sat down, held on tight again, and slipped down into the fork of the tree. Below, in the grass, the small pink dragon ran backwards and forwards, waving his tail.

'He's being encouraging,' said Grimmond. 'He's saying, "Come on, Robert. You can do it!" '

Robert came from the fork of the tree, sat on the lowest branch, and grasped the tree trunk with both his arms. For a moment he stayed there, for the fluttery feeling had come back into his tummy. Then quickly, he scrambled down and landed – FLUMP! – in the grass by the side of the small dragon. The small dragon blew six bubbles in his excitement. They were the biggest bubbles he had ever blown, and he looked at them in amazement as they floated off on the summer air. Then he jumped up, and ran after them. Already he had forgotten all about Robert and the tree.

Grimmond came down, and sat in the grass. Robert sat beside him. The fluttery feeling had gone from his tummy, and he felt all right. 'But I don't think I like climbing trees,' he said. 'I just wanted to be like James.'

Grimmond smiled at him. 'I like you better when you are just being Robert,' he said.

'So do I!' said Robert.

The trouble with dragons

The small, pink dragon had been living in the bush in Robert's garden for some time. All summer he had played happily on the lawn – but only Robert and Grimmond could see him. Robert knew this, because Maud thought that the dragon was as big as an elephant, and when she pretended to see him she gazed up to where she thought an elephant's eye would be. Robert's mother thought that he had the shape and size of a little dumpling, and when she pretended to see him, she crouched down to the ground. Robert's father said that he had never seen a dragon, and if he did he would run away as fast as he could.

In fact, the pink dragon was the size of a large dog, and was quite puppy-shaped about the tummy and paws, which seemed a bit too big for his body. Robert thought that it was a pity that other people couldn't see him, for he was so nice and funny to look at. The more Robert thought about it, the more he felt sure that he was the only child in the world with a dragon of his own – and the more he thought this, the more he wished that he could walk down the street with the pink dragon on a lead, for all to see.

Grimmond said that this was not a good idea. 'Don't even think about it! If you think about a thing often enough and hard enough, it some-times comes true,' he said. But Robert lay awake that night, and thought about the dragon as hard as he could. The very next day, people began to see bits of him. They never saw all of him, but the little bits they did see were quite enough to cause a great deal of confusion.

It began when Robert's Aunt Dorothy and Uncle George came for a visit. In the afternoon, Aunt Dorothy saw what she thought was a pink rose, peeping from the leaves of the bush. 'How beautiful!' she cried, as she hurried down the garden. In a short time she came back, looking rather pink herself; it makes you feel remarkably foolish to find that you have mistaken a nose for a rose. It is also very alarming.

'But whose nose was it, dear?' asked her husband.

'I'd rather not say,' said Aunt Dorothy – for the dragon's nose was not like any other nose she had ever seen, and she felt that if she described it, no one would believe her.

Aunt Dorothy went into the house, for a quiet lie down.

Uncle George went to the bush, and thrashed about inside, looking for the owner of the nose. Robert lay in the grass and laughed and laughed, for he knew that the small dragon had left the bush and was now sitting half asleep in the tree.

Uncle George was surprised to find the bush empty. 'It isn't like Dorothy to imagine noses,' he said. Then he went into the house, to make her a cup of tea and pat her hand. He was a kind man.

Everyone thought that that was the end of the affair of the nose in the bush – but the next day Uncle George's dog, Roger, saw what he thought was a pink, juicy sausage. It was the tip of the small dragon's tail, sticking out of the bush; and when Roger bent to stiff it, it reared up, and came down, smack! on his nose.

Roger ran yipping over the lawn, to where Uncle George and Aunt Dorothy sat side by side in deck chairs. He was very alarmed, for he had never come across a sausage which fought back. Uncle George tried to calm him by stroking his head, but it was to Aunt Dorothy that Roger turned, and held up a trembling paw.

After that, Aunt Dorothy and Roger took to wandering about together, which was something that they had never done before. They went for long walks round the garden, and thought about the nose in the bush and the fighting sausage. They understood one another, for strange things had happened to both of them. Uncle George was left sitting alone on the lawn – nothing strange had happened to *him*. Sometimes, as they went round the garden, Aunt Dorothy and Roger looked at Uncle George, as if to say, 'How nice to be a person to whom nothing strange has happened!'

The looks made Uncle George feel uncomfortable, although it was not at all his fault that he hadn't seen a bit of the pink dragon. He too began to wander round the garden, to see if he could see something strange. He found only quite ordinary things, which made him sad. So there were Aunt Dorothy and Roger feeling unhappy because they had seen something strange, and poor Uncle George feeling sad because he hadn't. Uncle George was also feeling lonely without his wife and his dog, and to pass the empty hours he composed a song about the good times he had had, not all that long ago. It was called *Jolly Dog Rog*! and he sang it to the music of a small guitar. It was a cheerful tune, but somehow, listening to his uncle sing made Robert feel mournful. It was all very odd and everything seemed to be getting more confused than ever.

'This is what happens when dragons start being seen,' said Grimmond. 'I told you not to think about it!'

But Robert still liked the idea of leading his dragon through the streets, and having everyone come to their door to look at him. He went on thinking about it as hard as ever, but all that happened was Maud saw the dragon's eyes, gleaming one evening from the depths of the bush. She had long suspected that something unusual was happening, and she marched down the garden, bellowing at the top of her voice,

'WHAT'S GOING ON?' Seeing something strange could never alarm *Maud*.

As she shouted, the eyes disappeared. Robert ran after Maud, wondering if the small dragon had closed his eyes, or merely left the bush. Having Maud bellow at you was enough to make anyone either close their eyes or leave their bush, or possibly do both, Robert thought.

He found the small dragon crouched under the leaves, with his tail over his eyes, and his paws over his ears. And it was clear that Maud couldn't see him, for she just peered into the bush, and said 'HUH!' and then marched away.

Robert and Grimmond went back over the

garden. Aunt Dorothy and Roger had at last got over their fright, and were sitting by Uncle George. Uncle George was smiling happily.

'All's well that ends well!' said Grimmond.

But Robert just sighed. 'It would have been nice if they had seen all of the dragon,' he said.

'Have you ever thought,' said Grimmond, 'That other people might have dragons that *you* can't see?'

Robert was surprised by this idea. 'Even Maud?' he asked.

'Especially Maud,' said Grimmond. They sat down side by side on the front door step and smiled at one another as they thought of Maud's dragon; without a doubt it would be a loud-roaring, fire-breathing dragon, and Robert felt quite glad that he couldn't see it. Perhaps Grimmond was right after all, he thought, and a dragon was something best kept to yourself, like a story you tell yourself at bedtime, so that you won't be afraid of the dark, or a song you have invented to cheer yourself up when you are feeling sad. Perhaps if you try and share these things, they are never quite your own again, and never quite the same.

'But *you* see the dragon,' he said to Grimmond.

'That's different,' said Grimmond. 'I'm Grimmond!' He got up and began to stroll away over the garden.

'Well, has everyone got a Grimmond then?'
Robert shouted after him – but Grimmond didn't
answer.

Robert sat on the door step and thought about
everyone in the world having their own dragon
and their own Grimmond. It was a good thought
(and one that is especially helpful to have if you
are feeling lonely). Before him, in the deck chairs
set out on the grass, Aunt Dorothy and Uncle
George sang a rousing happy chorus of *Jolly Dog
Rog*! Roger howled, as he sometimes did when
someone sang, and just above their three heads
the small pink dragon flew unseen.

Shopping

One day Robert went to the baker's shop, to buy a loaf of bread. Grimmond went with him. In his pocket he had a list of all the things he wanted to buy.

> A ball of string,
> A hive of bees,
> A ship with sails,
> A bag full of nails,
> A very large cheese,
> And a kite.

'You can't buy those things in a baker's shop,' said Robert. But Grimmond said that he could, and he would. He took out his shopping list, to read it again – but the wind snatched it from his hand, and blew it away. Grimmond said that it didn't matter; he could remember all that he wanted to buy. Robert heard him murmuring the list of things to himself, as he went along the street – a ball of string, a hive of bees, a ship with sails, a bag of nails, a very large cheese, and a kite.

But when they reached the end of the street, the list began to sound a little strange. 'A bag full of bees,' said Grimmond. 'And a very large nail.' It didn't sound right at all, thought Robert.

Robert and Grimmond went back, and began to look for the shopping list. They looked amongst the fallen leaves – but the list wasn't there. They looked in the litter bin, but all they found were sweet papers and old bus tickets.

Robert and Grimmond went to the baker's shop to buy the loaf of bread. The shop was warm, and smelled of gingerbread men. On the shelves were scones and buns and tarts, and little round cakes with pink icing.

Robert bought his loaf, and he and Grimmond began to make their way back home. As they went, they tried to remember all the things on Grimmond's list – but they couldn't. Grimmond looked at the loaf of bread in Robert's bag. 'It's very easy to remember *one* thing,' he said. 'But it's very hard to remember *six*.'

For the rest of the day Grimmond tried to remember the list of things he wanted to buy.

Robert watched as he wandered in and out of the bushes, a sad, green little figure in his tasselled cap.

Bedtime came, and still Grimmond had not remembered all the things he wanted to buy. Robert climbed the stairs to bed. He put his red boots side by side on the rug, and snuggled down beneath the blankets – and he was just about to fall asleep when the door of the loft was opened, and Grimmond looked down. 'I've remembered all the things on my list!' he said. 'Tomorrow I shall go to the baker's shop and buy them all.

> A ball of string,
> A hive of bees,

51

A ship with sails,
A bag full of nails,
A very large cheese,
And a kite.'

'I *told* you,' said Robert. 'You can't buy all those things in a baker's shop!'

But Grimmond had closed the door of the loft, and BOING! went the springs as he climbed into bed.

Cuckoo!

One day Robert went to stay with his grandmother. Grimmond went too, and even though she couldn't see him, Robert's grandmother said that she was pleased that Grimmond had come to stay. She shook up the cushion on the rocking chair, so that Grimmond could sit by the fire and rock. 'Tea is at four o'clock,' she said, and went into the kitchen to make the sandwiches and cut the cake.

Robert put the cloth on the table, and set out the tea cups, the milk jug and the sugar basin. Then he sat down on the rug, to wait for tea. *Creak-creak* went the rocking chair, as Grimmond rocked to and fro. *Tick-tick* went the clock on the wall. It was almost a quarter to four.

'I'm very hungry!' said Grimmond – but there were fifteen more minutes to wait until it was tea time.

Grimmond watched the little hand on the clock, but it didn't seem to move at all. So he climbed up on to a chair, to see if the clock was still going. He was very surprised when two little doors opened at the front of the clock, and a cuckoo dashed out. It bounced about on the end of a spring, and it shouted 'CUCKOO!' very loudly in Grimmond's ear. Then it dashed back inside again, and closed the doors – SLAM!

Grimmond was very annoyed. 'That wasn't very polite,' he said. 'Come back at once and apologize!' He knocked on the little doors, but the cuckoo didn't answer. He tried to open the doors, but they stayed firmly closed. 'He's bolted his doors,' said Grimmond. 'He's thoroughly ashamed of himself, and he's locked himself inside.'

Robert lay on the rug, and waved his red boots in the air, and laughed. 'It isn't a *real* bird,' he said. 'It's part of the clock.' But Grimmond wouldn't listen. He was going to stay on the chair, he said, and wait until the rude bird came out, and said that he was sorry. He stood there as Robert's grandmother brought in the sandwiches and the cake. And he stood and waited as the tea was poured into the tea cups.

'Please come down,' said Robert. 'It's time for tea. It's almost four o'clock.'

'Don't care!' said Grimmond. Then the little doors were flung open once more, and out dashed the cuckoo. 'CUCKOO!' he shouted, bobbing up and down in front of Grimmond's nose. 'CUCKOO! CUCKOO! CUCKOO!' he said. Then back he went, and SLAM! – the little doors were closed again.

Grimmond stepped slowly down from the chair. He straightened his hat. He whistled a little tune, and strolled twice round the table in a 'don't care!' sort of way. Then he sat down.

'Never mind,' said Robert. 'Have a sandwich.

Have some cake!' For he knew that it would be no use at all to try to explain about the bird in the clock. Sometimes Grimmond just wouldn't *listen*.

'Tick-tock,' said the clock, as everyone ate their tea. 'Tick-tock,' it said, counting off the minutes. And Robert wondered what would happen when it reached a quarter past four, and the little doors flew open, and the cuckoo came dashing out again.

The birthday

It was Robert's birthday, and he was five years old. All his birthday cards had the number 5 on them. Some said, 'You're 5 Today!' some said, 'Now you are 5!' and one card had a wonderful badge, with the words, 'I'm Five!' in big, yellow letters. Robert pinned the badge to his T-shirt, and went down to the bottom of the garden, to show Grimmond.

Grimmond was sitting in the bush with the small dragon, and at first he didn't understand what a birthday was. But when Robert explained everything to him, he became very excited, and said that he felt sure that today was his birthday too. 'How do you know?' asked Robert.

Grimmond said he knew because he had a

tickly feeling in his tummy, and because his ears were growing greener and more pointed. 'Isn't that what happens on your birthday?' he asked.

Robert said, well, yes . . . he *did* have a tickly feeling in his tummy; but his ears were just as they had always been. He felt them, to make quite sure, then he and Grimmond went for a walk round the garden, to talk about how strange it was that they should both have the same birthday. The small dragon trotted behind (funnily enough, he knew exactly when his birthday was – it was the first of March). As they went, Robert decided that when he went back to the house, he would ask Maud to make a special birthday card for Grimmond. Maud made very good Christmas and birthday cards.

'How old *are* you?' he asked, so that Maud could put the number on the front of the card.

'A hundred and two,' said Grimmond.

'*A hundred and two*!' said Robert. 'Are you sure? How do you know?'

Grimmond said that he was quite sure – that it had just come over him, all at once, that he was a hundred and two. And with that he trudged sadly back over the garden, sat down again in the bush, and began to grow himself a grey and woolly beard. At first it grew in gentle little wisps, like faint curls of smoke – but then it became thick and·heavy, and as prickly-looking as a hedge in winter.

Robert ran into the house, to ask Maud to make the special birthday card. 'And could you please put a very cheerful message in it?' he asked.

Maud got out her paints and brushes, and began to make the card at once. Robert went back to the garden. Grimmond was still sitting in the bush, and still growing the grey beard. It had now reached his feet, and was creeping, little by little, from the opening of the bush. It was, in its way, quite interesting, like a long, grey, woolly animal, and Robert almost forgot that it had anything at all to do with Grimmond, but for the doleful voice which came from the bush to remind him. 'A hundred and two! A hundred and two!'

Robert ran back to the house, but the birthday card wasn't ready. Maud curved her arm round it, so that he shouldn't see it until it was finished – but Robert knew that it was going to be very special, for Maud had got out some snippets of tinsel, which she had saved from the Christmas tree decorations, and a little glass flask, which was full of tiny specks of gold.

For the rest of the morning, Maud made the birthday card, Grimmond sat in the bush and grew his beard, and Robert played on the lawn with the small dragon. In the afternoon, Robert had his birthday party. All his friends arrived, and everyone had a wonderful time. Even the small, pink dragon joined in the games – although of course no one but Robert could see him. Sometimes, in the middle of all the shouting and the laughter, Robert thought of Grimmond, sitting alone in his bush. The thought made him sad, but it is impossible to stay sad when it's your fifth birthday, and all your friends and family are around you. Robert thought less and less of Grimmond as the day went on, until at last he forgot all about him, and just enjoyed the birthday party.

Then evening came, and one by one, the guests went home. Maud sat on the front door step, and put the finishing touches to Grimmond's birthday card. It was very beautiful, covered in snips of tinsel, and little golden specks, and the verse inside read, 'Hurrah for you! You're 102!'

'Thank you very much!' said Robert, and he carried the card carefully over the lawn. But when he reached the bottom of the garden, the bush where Grimmond sat was nowhere to be seen. In its place there stood what looked like a small, grey mountain. It was made entirely of beard, and already several small creatures were exploring it with some interest – a beetle and her family were preparing to climb up its side, a fieldmouse was sitting and wondering whether or not to make a nest at the foot, and a cloud of gnats danced at the top. The small dragon was sitting on a low branch of the tree, and gazing down in amazement – as well he might; for in the middle of the beard-mountain was Grimmond. Both Robert and the small dragon could hear him muttering to himself as he floundered about, trying to make his way outside.

Robert shooed the small creatures away. Then he put the card carefully down on the grass, took hold of the end of the beard, and began to roll it up. Round and round the bush he went, with the bundle of beard growing bigger and bigger, until at last he had to trundle it over the ground. The small dragon came down from the tree, but he wasn't a great deal of help. He got rather excited, as he trotted behind Robert, and this made his little, plump legs go suddenly in different directions, so that he fell down. The fall startled him, and he lay like a pink, surprised starfish, until Robert helped him to his paws again. As Robert bundled up the beard, and helped the small dragon, Maud sat on the doorstep, and from time to time shouted, 'HAS HE READ HIS CARD YET? DOES HE LIKE IT?' And Robert shouted back, 'NOT YET! HE'S STILL IN THE BUSH!'

It was, altogether, a very busy end to a birthday, but at last the bush came into view, and Robert saw Grimmond sitting in the opening, with his hat awry, and with a very sad look on his face.

It is hard to say whether it is more alarming or sad to find yourself completely buried by your own grey beard – or whether the whole thing isn't just rather funny. Robert didn't know whether to laugh or not. He crept into the bush, and sat by Grimmond's side. 'Why didn't you just magic it away?' he said.

'It wouldn't go,' said Grimmond sadly. 'It just kept on growing and growing.'

Robert looked at him. It is surprising to find that no matter how magical a person may be, there are times when they need the help of a friend. At the same time, it can seem quite an ordinary thing to discover that you yourself have a little magic power, that you have always had it, but had somehow forgotten about it. Robert held out his hand and took hold of Grimmond's green paw. 'Beard begone!' he said, in a loud, clear voice.

At once the beard detached itself from Grimmond's chin, and drifted over the garden, like a thunder-cloud. It was very strange – and even Maud saw it, for she shouted from the doorstep, 'COME IN AT ONCE! IT'S GOING TO RAIN!'

Robert and Grimmond smiled, for they knew that it wasn't going to rain. They came out from the bush, and Grimmond looked at his beautiful birthday card. He liked it very much. 'But I'm sure that you're not a hundred and two!' said Robert.

'No,' said Grimmond, 'I think that I'm ten. I *feel* as though I'm ten.'

'How does being ten feel?' asked Robert.

'Like being five,' said Grimmond, 'but twice as much.'

They made their way to the doorstep where Maud sat, and told her about the change in Grimmond's age. At first Robert thought that she would be annoyed, but she just grinned, and changed the 2 into a flower. The card now read, 'Hurrah for you! You're 10!' It no longer rhymed, but no one cared; they just sat on the doorstep, and watched the beard-cloud float off into the evening sky, growing smaller and wispier, until it couldn't be seen at all.

The voyage

Robert had been given a lot of presents for his birthday, but the one he liked best of all was a sailing ship, called *The Wanderer*. Robert felt that he couldn't wait to sail it on the pond, but by the time his birthday guests had left, it was evening, and the sky was growing dark. The next afternoon Robert and his father set out for the park. Grimmond went too.

The pond was in a pleasant spot, surrounded by trees. In the middle of the pond was a small, reedy island. No one lived there, except a family of moorhens. Whenever he visited the pond, Robert liked to watch the birds; but today he was far too excited to think of anything but the first voyage of *The Wanderer*.

He was so excited that at first he didn't notice that Grimmond was no longer wearing his jacket with the bright, brass button, but a striped sweater, and a long knitted cap – that on his feet were a huge pair of sea boots; on his shoulder was a brightly-coloured parrot; and over his left eye a black patch. As Robert gazed at this wonderful and colourful figure, Grimmond shrank until he was small enough to climb up the little rope ladder that hung over the side of the ship. Then he jumped down on to the deck, and waved his hand. Crouching by the edge of the pond, Robert heard the faint rattle of a chain, as the anchor was drawn up.

Robert ran to where his father sat on a bench, reading a newspaper. 'Daddy!' he said. 'Grimmond's sailing away on my ship!'

'That's nice,' said his father, from behind the newspaper.

'No, it isn't!' said Robert. 'If Grimmond's sailing away, I want to sail away too!' He ran back to the edge of the pond, and tried to make himself as small as Grimmond. He screwed his eyes tight shut, and thought hard about being small; but when he opened his eyes again, he was the same size as he had been before.

The Wanderer lay on the water, almost at his feet, but as Robert watched, the new, clean deck suddenly swarmed with tiny figures. They clambered about the rigging, and the sails filled with wind. They billowed beautifully, with a snapping, cracking sound. The wind also ruffled the water of the pond, and the prow of *The Wanderer* rose proudly, as it went forward to meet each little wave.

'I say!' said an elderly gentleman, who was passing by with his aged scottie dog, 'that's a fine ship you've got there!' He stood by Robert's side, and gazed out over the pond, but he didn't seem to see the tiny figures on the deck of the ship, or hear the sound of their sea-shanty. But Robert heard quite clearly. 'Oh, to Rio!' the crew of *The Wanderer* sang; and what can touch the heart with

67

sadness, like finding yourself to be the one who is left alone on the edge of the pond, at the end of a sunny afternoon. For you the day has almost ended, and all that lies ahead is suppertime and bed, while for others it's excitement and adventure.

Robert ran back to the bench. 'Daddy!' he said.

'Hmmm?' said his father from behind the newspaper; but it was impossible to explain about the spanking, billowing sails, and the rollicking sea-shanty.

At that moment, the weather changed. Dark clouds rolled over the sky, and the wind began to blow more strongly. The water of the pond rose in great, rolling waves, and *The Wanderer* was tossed up and down. Robert, his father and the elderly gentleman stood and watched as the ship rose high on each wave's crest.

'Most extraordinary!' said the elderly gentleman. 'She ought to have capsized by now. 'Why, you'd almost think she was manned, the way she's riding the storm!'

As they gazed in admiration at the little ship, she ran into the reeds that grew at the edge of the little island, and came to a halt.

'She's run aground!' said the elderly gentleman.

There was nothing that anyone could do. The pond wasn't very deep, but it was too deep for

either Robert or his father to wade across to the island. So it was decided that they would go home, and return with Robert's father's tall wading boots, which he wore when he went fishing, and a walking stick, to prod *The Wanderer* free from the mud and reeds. The elderly gentleman said he'd stay behind to keep an eye on the ship.

By the time Robert and his father returned to the park, it had begun to rain. Robert and the elderly gentleman stood and watched as Robert's father waded across the pond. The water rose up to his knees, and then almost to the top of his boots. When he could go no further, he reached out with the walking stick, and prodded *The Wanderer* free. At once, with a strong wind filling her sails, she skimmed round the island, and began to make for the further shore.

'Dash it – how exciting!' said the elderly gentleman, as he and Robert hurried to the other side of the pond. Robert's father came from the water, and followed them.

They were just in time to see the ship come to rest in the long grass at the water's edge. Her sails were tattered, and her decks were splashed with mud. Robert bent and picked her up. There was no sign of the little figures – nor was there any sign of Grimmond and his parrot.

Robert, his father, and the elderly gentleman and his dog began to make their way home. When they were halfway across the park, Grimmond appeared suddenly by Robert's side. His striped sweater and his long knitted hat were soggy with rain, his black eye patch had gone, his sea boots were caked with mud – and the less said about his parrot the better; except perhaps to remark that it was extremely bedraggled and very irate. But Robert was so glad to see Grimmond that he couldn't feel cross. He took told of his wet paw, and together they trotted home, behind Robert's father, the elderly gentleman and the scottie dog.

Heads down in the rain they went – but when they reached Robert's garden, the clouds lifted, and the sun came out. The elderly gentleman said goodbye, and he and his dog went off to their own house, a little way up the street. Robert's father went to put away the boots and the walking stick. Robert turned to Grimmond. He was now wearing his own brass-buttoned jacket and his woolly hat; and already his fur was drying in the sun, and he looked green and fresh and fluffy. There was no longer an irritable parrot on his shoulder, but above his head, on a branch of the tree, a fat brown thrush sat, singing merrily.

'Thank goodness for that!' said Grimmond.

Sadly, Robert climbed the stairs to his room, and put his ship on the windowsill. Only that morning she had been beautiful and new, and now she was battered and torn and dirty. Robert thought that he could never sail her again. But when he woke up the following morning, he found that *The Wanderer*'s sails had been mended and neatly furled, that her paintwork gleamed, and that her decks had been scrubbed clean. No one knew how this had come about (not even Grimmond, who said firmly that he wanted nothing more to do with ships). But there the vessel was, as good as new. Sometimes things happen which are quite unexplainable.

The picnic and the gingerbread men

One day, Robert and his family decided that they would go for a picnic in the wood. Robert went out into the garden, to tell Grimmond and the small dragon. They were sitting together on a branch of the tree, and they had never heard of a picnic. When Robert described what it was, they both became very excited. Grimmond scrambled down from the tree, and hurried off to the dragon's bush, to conjure up a picnic basket full of delightful food.

The small dragon stayed on the branch of the tree. He had closed his eyes, and a blissful look came over his face as he thought about the egg sandwiches, and cheese sandwiches, and the Bakewell tart that Robert had told him about.

Then, with his eyes still closed, he fell from the tree, as if in a swoon, lay flat on his back, and turned a pale shade of pink from sheer happiness. Who knows how long he might have stayed like this, had not Robert rolled him over on to his plump tummy.

The small dragon got to his paws, and together he and Robert went to where Grimmond was bustling about in the bush. The small dragon sat down in the opening, and snorted with excitement, and thumped his tail on the ground. Robert couldn't see what Grimmond was doing, but above the thumping and the snorting he could hear the creaking of a large wicker basket, and the chinking sound of china cups and plates.

'Egg sandwiches! Cheese sandwiches!' shouted Robert as loudly as he could, to remind Grimmond of what food to make for the picnic. 'Bakewell tart!'

He was beginning to sound like Maud – and in fact Maud herself came to the door and shouted, 'WHAT'S GOING ON?'

'I'm telling Grimmond what to put in his picnic basket,' said Robert.

'WELL, TELL HIM NOT TO FORGET THE GINGERBREAD MEN!' said Maud.

'DON'T FORGET THE GINGERBREAD MEN!' shouted Robert into the bush.

At this, the activity grew until every leaf and

twig quivered; and the small dragon thumped his tail so hard that little clouds of dust rose in the air.

Robert went into the house to get ready for the picnic. When he came out again Grimmond and the small dragon were waiting for him by the gate. They carried their picnic basket between them, and they both looked very smart. The buttons on Grimmond's jacket shone brightly, and the small dragon had a large ribbon bow tied round his neck.

All the way to the wood they talked about how wonderful the picnic would be, and the small dragon began to dribble from the corner of his mouth. He dribbled so much that Grimmond

changed the ribbon bow for a large bib. (The bib had the word *Tuesday* written on it, while the day was actually Wednesday, but that is by the by.)

When they reached the wood, Robert helped his mother spread the rug beneath the trees. Some little distance away, he saw Grimmond and the small dragon kneel and open the lid of their picnic basket. Then the small dragon said, 'HOO!' in a surprised tone of voice, reached into the basket and held up a crust of bread in his paw.

Robert went to see what was happening. Crouching by the wicker basket he looked over the side. There, sitting in Grimmond's neatly folded picnic cloth, were six little gingerbread men. One held a cherry and one a clump of icing – which was all that was left of the Bakewell tart. All had crumbs round their mouths (for they had also eaten the sandwiches) and all looked surprised; as well they might. Grimmond had only made them that morning, and all they had seen of the world so far was egg and cheese sandwiches, a Bakewell tart, and the inside of a picnic basket.

'Oh, Grimmond,' said Robert, closing the basket lid. 'They should have been *biscuits*.'

'Biscuits?' said Grimmond. 'No one said anything to me about biscuits!'

From inside the basket there came the sound of scuffling. Robert and Grimmond leant their elbows on the lid, and smiled and waved at

Maud, who sat under a tree, watching with narrowed eyes. True, she couldn't see Grimmond, the small dragon or the picnic basket, but she was very good at guessing about things, and always knew when she was right – even if you said, 'That isn't it *at all*!' And if she ever found out that Grimmond had made six little men, instead of gingerbread biscuits, she would never let the matter drop.

'WHAT ARE YOU DOING?' she shouted.

'Nothing!' said Robert. By his side, Grimmond tried to whistle in a carefree way. Inside the basket the sound of scuffling grew louder. Robert lifted the lid once more, and he and Grimmond and the small dragon looked inside.

The gingerbread men were sitting huddled together, and some of them were holding hands; which wasn't surprising. It can be very alarming (as well as delightful) to have golden sunshine pour down on your head, where before you have seen only little shafts of light, shining through the gaps of the wicker basket.

'Burp!' said the gingerbread men, who had eaten too much.

'Coo!' said the more thoughtful ones, as they gazed up at Robert, Grimmond and the small dragon.

Having said these short words, they looked at one another in delight. 'Burp!' and 'Coo!' were the first words the gingerbread men had ever spoken, and while they are not much, as words go, they do express how you feel when you have eaten too much, or have just seen your first small boy, your first Grimmond and your first pink dragon.

Then, with surprising speed, they scrambled from the basket, and, still keeping close together, began to make their way down the path. They Burped and Cooed to one another as they went, but soon they began to invent new and longer words, as they discovered grass, and trees, and earth, and stone, the facts that you can trip over stones and skin your knee, and that skinning your knee hurts.

In fact, they had learned quite a lot about the world by the time they reached the bend in the path. For a moment they stood there, bearing the skinned-kneed gingerbread man in their midst, then they whisked round the corner and were gone.

Robert and the small dragon watched them go. The small dragon thumped his tail on the ground, like a happy dog. Picnics were turning out to be far more interesting than he thought, and he decided that he liked this particular picnic very much – except for the loss of the sandwiches and the Bakewell tart. But he supposed that somehow Robert would supply him with more sandwiches and tart, and he leaned against Robert's shoulder in a trusting way, and dribbled down the Tuesday bib.

But Grimmond had pulled his hat down over his eyes, and was sighing loudly. Robert took hold of his paw, and led him gently back down the path. It must make you very sad, he told himself, to have made six little persons, and to have them merely say 'Burp!' and 'Coo!' to you, before running off into the wide world.

But then, Robert thought, as they made their way to where the family sat smiling under the trees, he could simply be sad because they had eaten his picnic.

Sometimes, with Grimmond, it was hard to tell.

Grimmond's family

Grimmond and the small dragon went to sit by their empty picnic basket. They spread their cloth under a tree, but there was nothing at all to eat. Robert went to sit by Grimmond's side, to try to cheer him up. 'Couldn't you make another picnic?' he said.

'Oh, very well,' said Grimmond, and with a limp wave of his paw, he conjured up a most depressing pile of thin, damp sandwiches. They were not at all as picnic sandwiches should be, made from thick, nutty brown bread, and with lots of good filling, and a nice frill of lettuce peeping out round the crust. In fact they were so awful that the small dragon carried them one by one behind the tree, where he dug a little hole and buried them.

'Well, really!' said Robert. 'You can do better than that!'

'Yes, I can,' said Grimmond, 'but somehow my heart isn't in it. Somehow a picnic's not the same when you don't have your family round you.'

'Couldn't you conjure them up by magic?' asked Robert.

Grimmond said he wasn't sure; it was one thing to conjure up a parrot, and a striped sweater, but a whole family was quite a different matter.

'Try!' said Robert.

So Grimmond tried. He closed his eyes and murmured a spell softly to himself. At first he conjured up nothing more than little clouds of green mist, which drifted slowly over the clumps of fern and grass. Then the mist rose in columns, and formed itself into figures. One by one, the members of Grimmond's family came stepping out from between the trees.

'Oh, Grimmond, what a lovely family!' said Robert, as the members stood in little groups by the edge of the picnic cloth, glancing shyly at Robert.

But this peaceful state of affairs did not last. Grimmond's family soon felt at ease, and began to chatter to one another and to Robert.

Grimmond's Uncle Gwillam completely re-organized Grimmond's picnic arrangements. At the sight of his family Grimmond had at once conjured up plates of wonderful sandwiches. Uncle Gwillam had the cloth spread under a different tree, and gave orders as to exactly where the sandwiches should be set. 'Egg to the left! Cheese to the right!' he shouted.

'He was in the army, dear,' Grimmond's aunt Lou-lou whispered in Robert's ear, by way of explanation, 'After tea he'll make us all go on a long refreshing march!'

She gave a small sigh, but Robert thought that a march might be rather fun. (Just what a march with Uncle Gwillam was like he was yet to discover!)

Grimmond's mother and father sat one on each side of Robert, and talked about their son. They were very proud of him. 'He has come up in the world!' said Grimmond's father.

'Indeed he has!' said Grimmond's mother, 'Why, he lives in a loft, and you can hardly get much higher than *that*.'

Grimmond's grandmother was as round and green as a little apple, and she carried a large handbag. She saw at once that the small dragon was wearing the wrong bib, and that it was damp. Delving in the bag she brought out a bib which had Wednesday written on it. She was the kind of grandmother who always has the right thing to hand. When she had tied the bib round the small dragon's neck, she brought from her bag a ball of

wool, and a pair of knitting needles, and began to
make him a pair of mittens and matching socks, to
keep him warm when winter came – for she was
the kind of grandmother who looks ahead.

Grimmond's aunt Tishy, however, was the
kind of aunt who always looks back. She cried a
lot, and dabbed at her eyes with a little lace-edged
handkerchief. She told Robert a very long story
about a certain Mr Minto, who wore a bell on his
hat and whom she was to have married; but who
instead went on a long sea voyage, and sent her a
postcard which read, 'You are ever in my
thoughts.' On the other side of the postcard was a
picture of the volcanic mountain, Popocatapetle.

82

This story made Robert feel quite drowsy, and he would have fallen asleep, had it not been for two of Grimmond's cousins, who rolled about in the grass close by. 'A *bell* on his *hat*!' they said, snorting with laughter.

To have her romantic story turned into a comic tale made Tishy weep harder than ever, and she rushed off between the trees. Grimmond's grandmother sent several other cousins after her, and they scuttled off, calling her name loudly.

Grimmond's grandfather leant against a tree trunk and dozed – although he opened an eye when any of his family, or Robert, passed by, and patted them with a broad and heavy paw; which was his way of saying, 'I love you – be happy!'

Then Grimmond's uncle Griff began to play his musical instrument. It was rather like a large banjo, and it made a strange plunking sound, which seemed slightly out of tune. But all the family liked it, and all joined in the chorus of the song, singing the words loudly, and waving their paws in the air. Even Tishy came back, dry-eyed and smiling, and all but one of the cousins who had been sent to look for her.

The cousin who didn't return was called Chumley, and he was known for his boldness and sense of adventure.

'Although, dear,' Aunt Lou-Lou whispered in Robert's ear, 'he hasn't quite *had* an adventure yet, as he is considered to be too young.'

At this, Grimmond's grandfather opened both eyes, and said, in a booming voice, 'Nonsense! If a body *wants* an adventure, it means he is old enough to *have* an adventure.'

So it was decided that Chumley should be allowed to go his own way for a little while. A lot of families have someone who is wild and free; who does not always do the usual thing, but, like Mr Minto sticks a bell on his hat and sails away to South America. (Not all families are as understanding about this as was Grimmond's family, however.)

In the middle of this discussion of the wild free Chumley, Aunt Tishy's tears, the playing of Uncle Griff's banjo, the knitting, the talk and the laughter, no one stopped eating, and drinking, and Grimmond never stopped conjuring up plates of sandwiches, and flasks of hot, sweet tea. But at last everyone was full, and it was time for the march!

Uncle Gwillam ordered everyone to stand in line, two by two. Robert, Grimmond and the small dragon were kindly allowed to make a small party of three at the end of the procession, as they did not wish to be separated.

At first, it was just a rather brisk march, and Robert, Grimmond and the small dragon had no trouble in keeping up. But soon the family began to go faster and faster, as they in turn tried to keep up with Uncle Gwillam. This was not easy, as not only did he move very quickly, he also went over or through things, rather than round them. 'Nothing stands in his way, dear!' cried aunt Lou-Lou, as everyone plunged into a patch of thick bushes. When they came out at the other side, they were almost at the edge of the wood. The trees had thinned out, and the ground sloped down to a ditch. Beyond the ditch was a flat, brown field.

Robert, Grimmond and the small dragon stood and watched the family go flying down the slope and over the ditch. They jumped with great whoops, and the aunts Tishy and Lou-Lou were the last to go; their shawls floated out behind them as they went, and Robert caught a glimpse of their shiny, black button boots. Then over the field the family ran, no longer two by two, but scattered, like a flock of bright green birds.

Robert, Grimmond and the small dragon made their way back to where Robert's own family waited for him beneath the trees. The picnic baskets were packed, and slowly, everyone began to make their way home. The small dragon was so sleepy that he had to be carried. Robert held his head and shoulders, and Grimmond held his back legs and tail. The bit in the middle dropped a little, but he didn't seem to mind. In his paw, he carried the matching mittens and socks made for him by Grimmond's grandmother.

When they reached the garden they set him down, and he toddled off to his bush, blowing spit-bubbles as he went. They were the biggest and most beautiful bubbles he had ever blown, and as they drifted over the garden, there, reflected in each bubble, was the tiny picture of a tired but happy family. Then – pop! – the bubbles vanished; but the family remained, as loving families do.

Robert thought of Grimmond's family, trotting home in the dusky light. They would be going down a lane, with fragrant hedgerows high on either side. Two by two and arm in arm they would go, with the plink-plink of Uncle Griff's banjo, Aunt Tishy's sniffs, and the booming voice of Grimmond's grandfather, making a reassuring sound in the gathering night.

In his bush, the small dragon blew one last string of bubbles before he fell asleep. They bowled over the lawn, and even Maud saw them. 'Someone's blowing bubbles,' she said. 'They're sitting on their back door step, blowing bubbles because they're feeling happy.'

And at this, Robert smiled – for, as so often happened with Maud, she was very nearly right.

School

Maud was going to school for the first time. She was very pleased and excited, and she hurried round the room, looking for things to put in her new school bag – pencils and crayons, and a big, red apple. Robert sat on the bottom stair and watched her. Grimmond sat by his side. 'I'm going to go to school, too!' he said.

Robert looked at him. '*Can* Grimmonds go to school?' he asked.

'They can if they want to,' said Grimmond, and straight away he conjured up a big, blue school bag for himself. Inside it was everything that Grimmond owned – his umbrella, his kite and ball of string, and his yellow telephone. With his bag over his shoulder, he scampered along the

path, behind Maud and her mother.

The small, pink dragon saw them from the bush, and he trotted out, blowing spit-bubbles of excitement. 'He says that he wants to go to school too,' said Grimmond, and he conjured up another blue school bag, which the small dragon hung round his neck. Then through the gate and down the street they went. Robert followed, feeling rather sad, and a little bit lonely. Robert himself was going to school fairly soon – and he wasn't at all sure that he would like it.

The school was a big, red-brick building which stood at the corner of the street. Sometimes when Robert and his mother passed by, the playground was full of shouting children. 'What fun you will have when you go to school, Robert,' said his mother. But Robert didn't think that he would have fun. He liked being at home, with all the things and people he knew around him.

Now, they reached the playground, and Maud marched right across it, up to the big school door. Maud was always brave and bold, and liked to do things by herself. Grimmond and the small, pink dragon scampered behind her. The school bell rang, and everyone went inside.

Robert and his mother went home. Robert felt more lonely than ever. There was no sign of Grimmond to be seen – not his umbrella hanging from a branch of the tree, or his kite and ball of string lying in the grass – for he had taken all these things with him. And the nest that the small, pink dragon had made for himself was completely empty, with not even a pink dragon-scale left to show where he had been.

For the rest of the morning, Robert played sadly by himself. Then, in the middle of the afternoon, he went with his mother to bring Maud home.

Out she came from the big school door, smiling and swinging her bag. Behind her came Grimmond and the small, pink dragon, tumbled head over tail by the running feet of the children. But they didn't seem to mind, for they too were smiling.

Everyone began to make their way home, chattering happily. Maud talked to her mother, and Grimmond and the pink dragon whispered and giggled together. Robert walked sadly behind. Everyone had been to school, and had a wonderful time – but he still didn't think that he would like it at all.

After tea he went out into the garden, and sat down beneath the tree. Grimmond came and sat beside him. 'What's the matter, Robert-The-Boot?' he asked.

'I don't ever want to go to school!' said Robert.

'But school is fun!' said Grimmond. 'It's fun to do things with other people. It's fun to learn new things. And it's fun to run round the playground, shouting and laughing.'

Robert lay back in the grass, and looked at Grimmond. He seemed very happy after his day at school. 'Perhaps I might like it after all,' said Robert – for he knew that whatever Grimmond told him was the truth.

'And I shall go with you,' said Grimmond. 'I shall make myself as small as a mouse, and hide in your pocket.'

'Will you?' said Robert. 'Will you *always* be with me? Even when I'm grown-up?'

'If you want me to,' said Grimmond.

'I shall always want you for my friend!' said Robert.

Then they jumped up, and with the small, pink dragon, they ran round and round the garden, making as much noise as a whole playground full of shouting children.

The trouble with
long words

One day, Robert went to the library with his sister
Maud. Grimmond went too. Robert had often
been to the library, but Grimmond had never
been before. He *said* that he was very pleased to be
going – but when he got inside, he looked at the
books on the shelves, and then he sat down on a
little chair and pulled his woolly hat over his eyes.

'What's the matter?' asked Robert.

Grimmond said that he couldn't find a book
that he liked. So Robert looked along the shelves,
and at last he found a book which he thought
would be just right. It had a picture of a mole on
the cover, and pictures of moles inside. There
weren't a great many words on the pages, but
Robert could read some of them. He was very

pleased. He took the book to Grimmond, and sat down beside him, and read 'Mole' and 'Hole' and the title of the book, *The Mole in the Hole*.

But Grimmond said that he didn't like the book. What he wanted, he said, was a book full of long words, like 'Thursday' and 'Marmalade' and 'Walkingbackwards' and 'Bus station'.

So Robert went back to the shelves and found a big book, full of long words. Grimmond took off his hat, opened the book and began to read, very quietly, to himself – wsp-wsp-wsp. . . .

'Which words say "Thursday" and "Marmalade"?' asked Robert. Grimmond said that he didn't know.

'How do you know what the story's about, if you can't read the words?' said Robert. But Grimmond pretended not to hear him, and turned the pages of his book.

Robert sat beside him, and looked at the book about the mole. The pictures told the story – but it was lovely to be able to look at the words, and know which ones said 'hole' and which said 'mole'. Robert decided that he would take the book home, so that his mother could read all the other words to him.

Grimmond said that he would take his book home too, and read it all by himself.

'What's the use of a book if you can't read all the words?' said Robert. Grimmond said that he didn't care – he *liked* a book full of big, long words.

But, that night, as Robert lay in bed, he heard the sound of rustling pages, and the sound of Grimmond's voice, as he tried to read his book. 'Thursday,' he said, 'Walkingbackwards and Marmalade.'

Then, 'Oh, bother. . . !' he said, and – THUMP! – the book full of long words was dropped to the floor.

A new friend

One day, a visitor came to spend the afternoon, and have tea at Robert's house. With her she brought her little boy, who was called Matthew. Matthew was just the same age as Robert. He had freckles, and he laughed a lot, and Robert liked him as soon as he saw him. He took Matthew into the garden, and showed him the tree that he, Robert, had once climbed. He pointed out the high branch where he had sat. It looked higher than ever. Robert hoped that Matthew wasn't going to say, 'Let's climb up!'

But Matthew just looked at the branch, and then at Robert. 'Did you really climb up there!' he said. 'I don't like climbing trees.'

'Neither do I!' said Robert. Then he took

Matthew to the secret place behind the shed. Matthew liked the secret place a lot. Robert was very pleased. It is always pleasant to make a new friend, especially when they like the things that you like, and don't like the things that you don't like.

After Matthew and Robert had stayed in the secret place for a while, they came out. Matthew sat on the lawn, and Robert went into the house to get some of his toys. He put them in a big cardboard box – and he had just dragged the box out to the front step, when he saw that Grimmond and the small, pink dragon were standing on the edge of the lawn, gazing at Matthew. Then, paw in paw, they went a little nearer and a little nearer, until they stood right in front of him. 'HOO!' said the small dragon. Grimmond made a low bow, and said, 'How do you do!' But Robert knew that Matthew could neither see nor hear them.

'Silly old Grimmond!' he said, as he dragged the box over the lawn.

'Indeed!' said Grimmond, and he turned and stalked off, with the small dragon behind him.

Robert watched as Grimmond and the small dragon went into the bush. Then he tipped the box of toys out on to the grass. There were lots of bricks for building things, a red fire engine, and a cassette recorder that had a tape of all Robert's favourite tunes.

Robert and Matthew played with the toys all afternoon. They built a great castle with the bricks, pretended that the castle had caught fire, and raced the fire engine over the lawn to put the fire out. Grimmond and the small dragon watched all this from the bush.

When Robert and Matthew were tired of running about, they lay on the grass and played the cassette tape. From the corner of his eye, Robert could see how the small dragon had come from the bush, and was dancing to the music. He looked funny and nice as he danced – but Grimmond, Robert saw, was still sitting in the bush. He looked smaller and greener, and he had pulled his hat down until it almost covered his eyes. Then Robert forgot all about Grimmond and the small dragon, for his mother came from the house, carrying a tray. On the tray were sandwiches, mugs of milk, and two bowls of red wobbling jelly.

It was lovely to have tea on the lawn with a friend. When Robert and Matthew had finished eating, it was time for Matthew and his mother to go home. He said, 'I've enjoyed myself a lot!' and Robert said, 'Please come again!' He waved to the guests as they closed the garden gate behind them, then he began to pick up his toys, to put them back in the box.

As he did so, the small, pink dragon came over

the lawn, to sniff at an empty jelly bowl. When he raised his head, there was a little blob of jelly, quivering on the end of his nose. Robert laughed – but the small, pink dragon stood very still and quiet.

'What's the matter?' asked Robert. He tickled the small dragon's tummy, but the small dragon didn't cry 'HOO!' or blow bubbles. He just flopped down in the grass, and put his nose on his paws. Grimmond came from the bush, and stood by the small dragon's side. He looked very small and green.

'You forgot all about us!' he said to Robert. 'You didn't say "Here are my friends, Grimmond and a small pink dragon." '

'But Grimmond,' said Robert, 'Matthew couldn't see you.'

'He might have seen us, *if you had introduced us*,' said Grimmond.

Robert sat down in the grass beside the little dragon, and thought very hard. Matthew was a good friend – he liked all the things that Robert liked, the secret place behind the shed, building castles and racing the fire engine over the lawn. So perhaps Grimmond was right. If Robert had said, 'Here is my friend Grimmond,' Matthew might have been able to see him – and if he could see Grimmond he would surely be able to see the small dragon as well.

'Grimmond, I'm sorry,' said Robert. 'The next time that Matthew comes to play, I'll introduce you.'

At this, Grimmond became his right size and colour again, and the small dragon sat up, and blew a whole string of spit-bubbles. 'He says, "Thank you, and don't mention it, and please can he have some red, wobbling jelly?" ' said Grimmond.

So Robert went into the house for some more red jelly. He brought it in three bowls – one for Grimmond, one for the small dragon, and another one for himself; for what can be nicer than tea on the lawn with your very special friends?

The kite

One bright and windy afternoon in autumn, Robert went to the park to fly his kite. Maud, and Robert's grandmother went too, but Grimmond was nowhere to be seen. So Maud kindly wrote a note for Robert to leave, propped by the back doorstep. The note explained where Robert had gone, and what he was doing – and to make sure that Grimmond understood, Robert drew a little picture of himself, standing on the top of the little hill in the park, with the kite bobbing about above his head.

Then, to make sure that Grimmond understood that flying a kite was a *pleasant* thing, he ran back and drew a big smile on the face of the little figure of himself.

'Oh, come *on*!' said Maud. Mostly she was very understanding about Grimmond, but sometimes she got quite impatient. She set off over the garden, and Robert ran after her.

The small dragon was half asleep in his bush, but he opened an eye as Robert went by. He thought the yellow and red kite was beautiful, and he was most interested in the long tail, which dragged along in the grass. At first he thought that it was a whole procession of yellow and red butterflies, and wondered if he might be allowed to join in on the end – then he saw that the tail was part of the kite, and he put out a paw, shot out a claw, and broke six inches off the end. He felt very pleased and excited, for he had only recently discovered that he had claws and that they could be very useful. (But mostly he kept them tucked in his paws.) He sat and stared at the piece of kite-tail, with its two little yellow bows, and wondered what one could do with such a delightful object.

When Robert reached the park, he ran up the side of the little hill. His yellow kite bobbed behind him. When he reached the top, the kite rose up in the air. Robert let out some more kite-string, and sat down in the grass.

It is very pleasant, to sit on the top of a hill by yourself, with a friendly kite bobbing about high above your head. It is especially good when you can see members of your family close by. Robert gazed down to where his grandmother sat on a bench, sewing and talking to a friend. Maud was in the playground. She was swinging, and from where he sat Robert could hear the creak of the swing-chains as she swung to and fro. Higher and higher she went; much higher than Robert ever dared to go. Sometimes he wondered if he would ever be as brave and bold as Maud.

As he sat, and felt the pleasant tug of his kite-string, and pondered about being brave, he became aware of another kite, which was slowly making its way up the hill towards him. It was yellow and blue, and holding it firmly on either side were two fluffy green paws. 'Grimmond!' said Robert. He was very pleased to see him, and he thought that the kite was beautiful. 'I'll show you how to fly it,' he said, for he felt sure that Grimmond had never flown a kite before.

But Grimmond just flopped on to his back, and magicked the kite straight up into the air. 'That's not the way to do it!' said Robert – for there was none of the excitement of feeling the kite catch on a current of air, and go soaring up into the sky. Nor did Grimmond have a ball of kite-string, but just seemed to spin string from the end of his paw, rather like a spider spins a strand of web.

'It's the way *I* fly a kite,' said Grimmond, firmly. '*My* kite will go much higher than your kite. *My* kite will go higher than any kite has ever been before. *My* kite will go to the moon!'

And with that he yawned, and closed his eyes. The magical kite-string continued to spin out from the end of his paw, and the kite went higher and higher. By the middle of the afternoon it was just a tiny speck in the sky. And then it couldn't be seen at all.

Tea time came and shadows began to creep from beneath the trees. Robert's grandmother put her sewing away in her bag. The creak creak of the swing-chain ceased, and Maud came trotting along the path. Robert began to wind up his kite-string, and soon his kite came swooping down from the sky, and landed at his feet with a friendly rustling sound.

But there was no sign at all of Grimmond's kite, even though he was winding up the string as fast as he could. Robert's grandmother and Maud began to stroll slowly along the path, to the park gates. 'Wait for me!' Robert shouted, and they turned and waved to him and then went on, thinking that he would run down the hill and catch them up.

'Please, Grimmond! Hurry up!' said Robert. 'Everyone's going home for tea!'

'I'm being as quick as I can!' said Grimmond. He peered up into the sky, but the beautiful blue and yellow kite was still nowhere to be seen. Below the hill, Robert's grandmother and Maud were almost hidden in the early evening shadows

– and soon they would turn the bend in the path, and be completely lost from sight. Robert began to feel afraid. Was it possible, he thought, that they had forgotten about him, and were about to leave him, alone with a green, boastful creature, who had flown his kite to the moon, and now couldn't get it back again? He began to run down the hill, shouting, 'I'm still here – wait for *me*!' Then he stopped and looked back at the little figure, winding his kite-string as fast as his little green arms would allow. Grimmond's haste was making him careless and loops of string were falling about his feet. Robert felt very sorry for him, and wanted to go to him to say something comforting, but he still felt afraid. He stood on the side of the hill, not knowing whether to run down to his family, or up to his friend. It was impossible to decide what to do. So he took a deep breath, and shouted as loudly as he could: '*MAUD*!'

Maud heard him clearly, and came to him at once. As quickly as he could, Robert told her about Grimmond's kite, and of how he had flown it to the moon.

'I see!' said Maud, and she went back to where her grandmother was just disappearing round the bend in the path.

How brave she was, like an army with banners! thought Robert, as he watched her go marching along.

He went back to the top of the hill, where Grimmond was still winding the endless ball of string. From where he stood, he could see, beyond the park railings, streets of houses, with lights coming on in the kitchens, as children arrived home for tea. Soon he would be in his own bright kitchen, and the whole business of Grimmond's kite would be forgotten. Perhaps bravery is catching, like measles, for he was no longer afraid, but felt as bold as a lion. It was a wonderful feeling. 'Silly old Grimmond!' he said (but in a kindly way). 'Do stop winding string!'

'I can't!' said poor Grimmond. 'Sometimes, when you start doing something, you have to go on doing it, whether you want to or not.'

At that moment, there came the sound of voices, and over the prow of the hill came Maud and Robert's grandmother. Maud was carrying the scissors from Grandmother's sewing bag, and she marched to Robert's side, holding them carefully in front of her.

'Where is it?' she said, in her loud, confident voice; and when Robert pointed to the magical kite-string, she opened the scissor blades and cut it – SNIP!

'And that,' said Maud, with a grin, 'is that!'

She went back down the hill with her grand-mother, but Robert and Grimmond stayed on the hill-top for a little longer. Grimmond gazed sadly

at the end of the kite-string, which he still held in his paw. Robert gazed up at the sky, and thought of the big blue and yellow kite, lying amongst the grey rocks of the moon. It would make a lovely splash of colour, and it would certainly surprise any visiting astronaut. 'Perhaps he'll play with it,' Robert said to Grimmond.

The idea of an astronaut flying his kite cheered Grimmond up a lot, and he went off down the hill quite happily. Robert ran to join Maud, and hand in hand they went along the path to the park gates.

It was nice, holding hands with Maud; her fingers felt strong and warm, and she swung their two arms back and forth as they went.

'Sometimes, you're a nice person to have for a sister,' said Robert.

Then they reached the house, and the light came on in the kitchen, and lit up the bush where the small dragon was curled up fast asleep, with the two yellow bows held fast in his paw.

He had spent a puzzling day, for he hadn't been able to discover anything that he might do with a piece of kite-tail. But despite this, he slept happily – for he felt sure that in the morning Robert would explain exactly what one could do with two little bows, and that whatever it was, it would be something wonderful, and exciting.

'I don't want to go to bed'

It had been a wonderful summer's day, the kind you wish might never end. Robert had been playing ball with Grimmond and the small, pink dragon, but now it was growing dusk. Night was falling, and the garden seemed bigger, and very mysterious. It was the best time of all for playing at hide and seek. Robert found a special, secret place, behind the garden shed. There was just enough room for him to squeeze in between the wall of the shed and the fence – and there he sat, half-covered with great fronds of bracken.

It was a very long time before Grimmond and the small dragon found him. 'Well done, Robert-The-Boot!' said Grimmond. 'But now it's time for bed.'

'I don't want to go to bed,' said Robert. 'Make something exciting happen!'

'What exciting thing?' asked Grimmond.

Robert thought for a moment – then, 'Fireworks!' he said. 'Make some fireworks!' It would be wonderful, he thought, to see rockets go soaring up into the night sky. But although he tried as hard as he could, Grimmond couldn't conjure up any fireworks. Not even a sparkler for the small dragon to hold in his paw.

It was very puzzling, and the three of them sat in a row behind the shed, to think why Grimmond's magic wasn't working. As they sat, they heard Robert's mother come to the door. 'Robert!' she called. 'It's time for bed.'

'I don't want to go to bed,' said Robert to Grimmond. 'I don't feel sleepy at all. Please make something exciting happen.'

So Grimmond tried again. 'Suppose I turn the garden into a ship,' he said, 'with the shed as the cabin, and the fence the railing round the ship's deck.'

Robert said that he would like that very much. If Grimmond turned the garden into a ship, they could sail off over the night sky, and he need never go to bed again, if he didn't want to. He explained what was going to happen to the small dragon, and the small dragon blew two dozen spit-bubbles with excitement.

But, although Grimmond tried as hard as he could, the garden didn't turn into a ship, and the three of them stayed just where they were. 'Grimmond, what has happened?' said Robert.

'I think I'm too sleepy to make any magic,' said Grimmond. By his side, the small dragon made a snuffling sound. 'He says that he's sleepy too,' said Grimmond.

Robert looked at Grimmond and the small dragon. Their heads were nodding, and their eyes were almost closed. Looking at them made Robert feel very drowsy – and he had just fallen asleep when Maud came to the kitchen door. 'ROBERT!' she shouted, in her loud voice. 'IT'S TIME TO GO TO BED!'

At this, everyone woke with a start, and came from behind the shed. They could see Maud standing in the light which shone from the kitchen door. But the bottom of the garden was now quite dark, and Robert knew that she hadn't seen him come from the special place, and that it was still a secret.

Over the lawn he went with Grimmond and the small, pink dragon. When he reached his bush, the small dragon went inside at once, curled himself into a ball, and fell fast asleep.

'All good things come to an end,' said Grimmond, as he and Robert went on to the kitchen door.

But although he was sleepy, Robert didn't want his day to end. 'Not just yet!' he said.

So Grimmond rubbed his eyes with his green paws, took a deep breath, and made just one great rocket go up into the sky, high over the roof of the house. WHOOSH! it went, scattering coloured stars in its flight.

Robert stood and watched until the last star had faded away. Then, hand in paw, he and Grimmond climbed the stairs to bed.

BEAVER BOOKS FOR YOUNGER READERS

Have you heard about all the exciting stories available in Beaver? You can buy them in bookstores or they can be ordered directly from us. Just complete the form below and send the right amount of money and the books will be sent to you at home.

☐ THE BIRTHDAY KITTEN	Enid Blyton	£1.50
☐ THE WISHING CHAIR AGAIN	Enid Blyton	£1.99
☐ BEWITCHED BY THE BRAIN SHARPENERS	Philip Curtis	£1.75
☐ SOMETHING NEW FOR A BEAR TO DO	Shirley Isherwood	£1.95
☐ REBECCA'S WORLD	Terry Nation	£1.99
☐ CONRAD	Christine Nostlinger	£1.50
☐ FENELLA FANG	Ritchie Perry	£1.95
☐ MRS PEPPERPOT'S OUTING	Alf Prøysen	£1.99
☐ THE WORST KIDS IN THE WORLD	Barbara Robinson	£1.75
☐ THE MIDNIGHT KITTENS	Dodie Smith	£1.75
☐ ONE GREEN BOTTLE	Hazel Townson	£1.50
☐ THE VANISHING GRAN	Hazel Townson	£1.50
☐ THE GINGERBREAD MAN	Elizabeth Walker	£1.50
☐ BOGWOPPIT	Ursula Moray Williams	£1.95

If you would like to order books, please send this form, and the money due to:

ARROW BOOKS, BOOKSERVICE BY POST, PO BOX 29, DOUGLAS, ISLE OF MAN, BRITISH ISLES. Please enclose a cheque or postal order made out to Arrow Books Ltd for the amount due including 22p per book for postage and packing both for orders within the UK and for overseas orders.

NAME . . . .

ADDRESS . . . .

. . . .

Please print clearly.

Whilst every effort is made to keep prices low it is sometimes necessary to increase cover prices at short notice. Arrow Books reserve the right to show new retail prices on covers which may differ from those previously advertised in the text or elsewhere.